HORRIBLE HARRY
AND
THE DUNGEON

Acknowledgments

Special appreciation and thanks to . . .

My editor, Jane Seiter
My colleagues Val Vitalo, for her Human Bean Program, and Ellen Seeran, who shared her experiences in the Suspension Room

Dedicated with love to my second graders:

Arielle Celadon	Deanna Porter
Marissa DeAngelo	Nicole Primerano
Timothy Finkle	David Reyes
Colby Gaines	Michael Rice
Christine Hart	Jeffrey Seiser
Sean McDonnell	Ryan Smith
Daniel Merli	Ray Squires Jr.
Eric Mosakowski	Jacqueline Tribou
Christopher Mosher	Rannan Tyrrell
Christopher Pashley	Melissa Wallace
Amanda Pixley	Mark Woznicki
Katie Poole	

and to Emily Kline, my dedicated volunteer intern from February to June 1996

HORRIBLE HARRY
AND
THE DUNGEON

BY SUZY KLINE

Pictures by Frank Remkiewicz

SCHOLASTIC INC.

New York Toronto London Auckland Sydney
Mexico City New Delhi Hong Kong

MORE BOOKS ABOUT ROOM 2B

Horrible Harry in Room 2B

Horrible Harry and the Green Slime

Horrible Harry and the Ant Invasion

Horrible Harry's Secret

Horrible Harry and the Christmas Surprise

Horrible Harry and the Kickball Wedding

Song Lee in Room 2B

Song Lee and the Hamster Hunt

Song Lee and the Leech Man

ISBN 0-590-05946-7

36 35 34 33   2 3/0

Printed in the U.S.A.   40
First Scholastic printing, September 1998

Contents

The Dungeon

"Good morning boys and girls," the principal's voice said over the intercom. "Please stop what you're doing and listen. I have some bad news."

Bad news?

I stopped looking at a chrysalis hanging in our butterfly-net cage. Song Lee stopped drawing symmetrical butterfly wings.

Miss Mackle put down her book, *The Five Hundred Hats of Bartholomew Cubbins*. She was reading us the part where Bartholomew was about to get his head chopped off in the dungeon.

Harry kept playing pool on his desk. When he shot a small ball of clay with the eraser end of his pencil, Miss Mackle walked over and caught it.

Everyone in Room 2B looked at the little silver dots on the intercom box . . .

And waited for the principal to continue.

"Boys and girls, some children at South School are forgetting our school

rules. I know it's June. I know summer vacation is just two weeks away. But that's no excuse for bad behavior. From now on, any student who refuses to obey our school rules will—"

Mr. Cardini paused.

"—go to *the Suspension Room*."

Harry and I exchanged looks.

"I saw it," I whispered to Harry. "It looks like a prison. It's the old music room in the basement that smells. I know because the janitor told me. It just has cement walls. No windows."

Harry leaned over and whispered, "Hey Doug, let's call it the Dungeon."

"It's got to have a trapdoor if it's a dungeon," I said.

"Shhhh!" Miss Mackle shushed. Then she pointed to the intercom box on the wall.

"*If* you go to the Suspension Room,"

the voice continued, "you'll do your work there, eat there, and *sit there* all day. I've hired a teacher to supervise the Suspension Room. Mr. Skooghammer."

"Skooghammer?" I said. "His name sounds like a Viking weapon."

"Or an executioner," Harry said. Then he chopped a ball of clay in half with his ruler.

"Now," the principal added, "I want to end this message on a happy note. We are *also* starting a GOOD HUMAN BEANS bulletin board. Every time a student does something that is extra thoughtful and kind, a teacher will write it up on a green paper Bean and drop it in the Bean Box, and I will read it aloud each morning during our Bean Broadcast. The good beans will grow on our school beanstalk in the hall."

Harry blurted out, "If it's a real beanstalk, we have to make a giant for it that goes fe fi fo fum."

Song Lee giggled.

Mary made a face. "Harry, you'll never get a bean."

"Shhhh!" Miss Mackle put a finger to her mouth.

"Have a good day, boys and girls, and remember, be a good *Human Bean*."

When the intercom went off, Miss Mackle held up a pile of blank green beans. "I hope there are lots of these from Room 2B."

"I hate beans," Harry groaned. "They're the magical fruit. The more you eat, the more you toot."

When the class laughed, Miss Mackle folded her arms. "I can't believe that phrase is still around. Kids used to say that when *I* was in elementary school."

"How old are you, Miss Mackle?" Mary asked.

"I'll tell you my age, but you have to solve the math. Ready?"

I leaned forward.

Harry leaned back. He hates hard math problems.

"Eight plus eight, minus one, plus fifteen, minus two, plus three."

Just when I got the answer, Sidney shouted, "*Look!* A butterfly crawled out of its chrysalis!"

Everyone turned and looked at the giant yellow net cage that hung in the middle of the room. The butterfly was perfectly still. Its wings were pointing straight up.

Miss Mackle clapped her hands. "Look at our beautiful painted lady! Song Lee, you're my helper today. Please go get Mr. Cardini. Tell him we have good news in Room 2B."

As soon as Song Lee left the room, Miss Mackle made an important announcement. "Don't forget about this final stage of the butterfly. It needs time to dry its wings before it flies, so don't anyone jostle the net cage or touch a wing."

"Yes, Miss Mackle," we all said.

"What's the good news?" Mr. Cardini asked as he stood in the doorway.

"Look!" the class shouted.

"Your first butterfly! *Bravissimo!*" Mr. Cardini said. "What a miracle of life!"

Suddenly, the school secretary's voice came over the intercom. "Mr. Cardini?"

The principal went over to the silver box and pressed it once. "Yes?"

"Mr. Skooghammer just arrived. Shall I take him down to the Suspension Room?"

Everyone in Room 2B was pin quiet.

"Yes," Mr. Cardini replied into the silver box. "I'll get the two fifth-grade boys who will be joining him."

"The first two prisoners!" Harry whispered.

I nodded. "I wonder what Skooghammer looks like."

"I'll find out," Harry whispered back.

One minute later, Harry raised two

9

fingers. That means, May I go to the bathroom, please?

Miss Mackle frowned. "Can't you wait until I take the whole class down in fifteen minutes?"

Harry got out of his chair and jumped up and down. "It's a real emergency."

Mary made a face. "Harry will never get a bean. He's so gross!"

As soon as Miss Mackle gave Harry a nod, he took off.

While the rest of the class watched a second butterfly hatch, I watched the doorway. I couldn't wait for Harry to come back and tell me about Mr. Skooghammer and the Dungeon.

Mr. Skooghammer

I almost didn't recognize Harry when he showed up at the door. His hair was standing on end.

His eyes were bugged out.

When he walked over to his desk, he was shaking.

I looked back at the class. They were still watching the painted ladies.

Harry plopped down in his seat next to me.

"I saw him."

"Mr. Skooghammer?"

"*Mr. Skooghammer.*"

Harry's head clunked on the desk like a dropped bowling ball.

I looked at Harry's hair. It was wet. "What happened?" I asked.

When Harry turned his head, I noticed how big his black pupils were.

Just when he opened his mouth to speak, Miss Mackle made an announcement. "It's time now for our science clubs."

"What happened?" I repeated in a whisper.

"I'll tell you later. . . ."

I made a face.

I wanted to find out about Mr. Skooghammer now.

Song Lee, Mary, and Ida pushed their desks near the butterfly net. They were in the Butterfly Club.

Sidney and Dexter moved to a table for their Eagle Club. They had a huge framed picture of an eagle that Sidney brought from home.

Harry and I moved to the round table. We had twenty pages of notes about snakes. We were the Snake Club. Miss Mackle was waiting for us with her clipboard. It was our turn for a teacher visit.

"Why is your hair wet?" she asked Harry.

"I was hot so I cooled off a little."

"You know you're not supposed to get

your hair wet in the boys' bathroom sink."

"I didn't." Harry half smiled. "I got it wet in the drinking fountain."

"Harry!" Miss Mackle exclaimed. "I'm losing my patience with you and your antics."

I tried to change the subject. "See all the notes we took? Twenty pages."

Miss Mackle flipped through our folder. "Boys, I appreciate your hard work, but it's not necessary to copy every word out of the book. Be choosy. Copy only the facts that you think are *really* important about snakes."

When Miss Mackle moved on to the Dolphin Club, I scooted my chair closer to Harry's. "Give me the scoop about Skooghammer."

"He has a red beard."

"Yeah?"

"He's young and hairy."

"Hairy?"

"He was wearing Bermuda shorts, and I saw his legs."

"He has hairy legs?" I said.

"Yes, and . . ." Harry paused. "A big black shoulder bag. It bulges."

"What do you think is in it?"

"Maybe whips, a sledgehammer, and chains. It was heavy. I know because I tried to pick it up."

"You did?"

"I did."

"Where were you?" I asked.

"Downstairs in the basement. I watched him check out the Suspension

Room. Then he walked through the gym and into the boys' bathroom."

"You followed Skooghammer into the boys' bathroom?"

Harry nodded. "He left his black shoulder bag on the floor outside the stall. It was open a little, so I stuck my hand inside."

"Yeah, go on."

"That's when I pricked it on something sharp."

"Really?"

"It felt like that spiked weapon the knights used."

"A mace? Whoa!"

"Anyway, Skooghammer came out of the stall, so I dashed over to the sink and washed the blood off my fingers."

"Did you get a look at his face?"

"I sure did. The guy had an earring in his eyebrow."

18

"HIS EYEBROW?"

"Yup. His hair looked like a bunch of S.O.S. pads sitting on his head. The dude's weird. After Skooghammer went back to the Dungeon, I stuck my head in the fountain to cool off. I wouldn't want to spend a day with that guy."

"But I bet you'd like to see what's in his big black bag," I said.

Harry nodded. "I'm working on a plan."

"Really?"

"Yup, and when I figure one out, I'll raise my eyebrows three times. Just go along with whatever I need you to do. Okay?"

"Okay," I said slowly. But I wasn't looking forward to it.

Harry's Big Black Bag Plan sounded dangerous.

Clash, Flash, and the Big Black Bag Plan

That afternoon, while we were working on math, Harry kept rolling balls of clay and then chopping them in half with a ruler.

"I hate fractions," Harry whispered. "They're boring."

"You're making some right now," Miss Mackle said behind us. "Halves."

Harry took out his math paper. Not one problem was done.

"Would you rather work in the Suspension Room?" Miss Mackle suggested.

Harry suddenly got busy.

20

A few minutes later, I heard Mr. Cardini's voice at the door, so I looked up. He was standing there with a woman who was holding a camera. "Room 2B, this is Mrs. Kamaya, from the newspaper. I called her up so she could see the new butterflies and your interest in science."

As soon as the principal left, Miss Mackle went over to greet the woman. "Come in, Mrs. Kamaya. Boys and girls, we can have our science clubs meet now, if you like."

"Yeah!" Harry blurted out. "Take a picture of our Snake Club. It's the best!"

Sidney turned around. "Our Eagle Club is the best. We have better pictures. Besides, eagles eat snakes."

Harry put up a fist.

"Boys!" Miss Mackle exclaimed.

I could tell the teacher was embarrassed. She was rolling her eyeballs.

When she turned to the newspaper woman, she shook her head. "Welcome to the classroom. June is a challenge."

Mrs. Kamaya smiled. "I have three children. I know. They clash over the silliest things."

Harry walked over to Sidney and Dexter at the Eagle Club table. "Snakes eat eagles."

"Eagles eat snakes. The Mexican flag proves it!" Dexter replied.

Flash!

When Mrs. Kamaya took our picture, I noticed Miss Mackle had her hand over her eyes.

"Big deal," I said. "Eagles can't swim. Snakes can. Here's a picture of one."

Harry and I unrolled the mural we had made of a nine-foot-long sea snake.

Flash!

Dexter pulled a quarter out of his pocket. "Eagles are on coins and dollar bills."

Suddenly Song Lee waved everyone over to the butterfly net. "Look! The last painted lady just hatched. She's perfectly still on this branch."

Flash! Flash! Flash!

After Mrs. Kamaya talked with the Butterfly Club, Miss Mackle walked her to the door.

"Did you see new painted lady?" Song Lee said to Harry and me.

We looked.

"I put sugar water inside cage so butterfly can drink."

We watched Song Lee carefully lay a lid of sweet water down on the floor of the net cage.

"She is so beautiful," Song Lee said.

We nodded.

Then she did it.

Song Lee gently stroked one wing of the newest painted lady.

Harry and I gasped.

"You touched the butterfly wing!" I shouted. *"It could be handicapped now."*

Miss Mackle stepped back into the room. Mrs. Kamaya had just left. "What's going on?" she asked.

Song Lee started to cry.

"Who touched that butterfly wing?" Miss Mackle asked.

No one said anything.

"I just explained to everyone this morning about not touching the butterfly. That could keep the butterfly from flying!"

Song Lee was sobbing now.

"Who did this?"

Harry jabbed my side. When I looked at him, he was raising his eyebrows three times.

The Big Black Bag Plan!

I lowered my eyebrows. *WHAT?* I pantomimed.

Harry pantomimed back, *TELL HER I DID IT.*

Huh? I thought. Put the blame on Harry? How could I do that? He was my buddy. He was innocent.

I looked at Song Lee. She was still crying. I didn't want *her* to get in trouble.

Then Harry jabbed me and raised his eyebrows up and down again three times.

This was The Plan.

Slowly, I opened my mouth.

"Harry . . . did . . . it."

"Harry?" Miss Mackle replied.

"Yeah, I did it."

Song Lee looked up at Harry, and

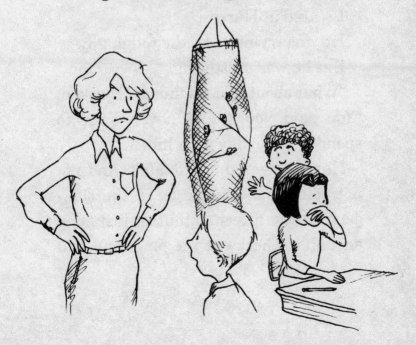

then wiped her eyes with her blouse sleeve.

"That's the last straw, Harry!" Miss Mackle said. "You will report to the Suspension Room tomorrow."

The Dungeon! I thought.

When Miss Mackle walked back to her desk to write a note to Harry's parents, Harry folded his arms. "I'll find out what's in Sk-skooghammer's black bag now."

I stared at Harry.

He was trying to be the tough guy.

But he was stuttering.

"What about Skooghammer?" I asked. "You said you would never want to spend a whole day with him."

Harry shivered. "I wouldn't. And I'm not going to. I plan to be in the Dungeon about fifteen minutes, just long enough to check out the place and find out what sharp weapons are in his bag. At 9:15, you tell Miss Mackle what really happened."

"You want me to rat on Song Lee?"

"No! Just tell the truth. Song Lee was out of the room when the teacher talked about the butterfly's wings. Song Lee won't be in trouble. She didn't know. Miss Mackle will feel bad, and come and get me."

Then Harry paused.

"Make that ten minutes in the Dungeon. Tell Miss Mackle at 9:10."

I shook my head.

Harry didn't know what he was getting himself into.

His Big Black Bag Plan depended on two important things.

Harry's bravery.

My tattling on Song Lee.

Neither was a sure thing.

Harry Goes to the Dungeon

The next morning Harry was not himself.

He came into Room 2B, sat down, and folded his hands.

He never does that.

"Are you okay?" I asked.

Harry nodded.

Then it came to me.

Harry wanted Miss Mackle to change her mind about sending him to the Dungeon.

I looked around the room. Song Lee wasn't there yet. I wondered if she was going to be absent.

Miss Mackle looked at the carnations on her desk. "Who brought these?"

Harry raised his hand. "I did. They're for the butterflies. They need pollen."

Then he flashed a toothy smile.

It was Harry's way of saying he was sorry about yesterday.

Miss Mackle smiled back. "How thoughtful! Thank you, Harry."

Everyone watched Miss Mackle snap the heads off the three carnations and place them on the floor of the butterfly cage.

Two painted ladies landed on them right away. We watched them sniff the petals.

A minute later, when Mr. Skooghammer appeared at the doorway, the entire class turned to look.

"Man, he's weird," Dexter whispered behind me.

Some other kids whispered about the
earring in his eyebrow. I noticed his
S.O.S. pad hairdo.

Then I noticed Harry.

His folded hands looked like an air
drill hammering on his desk.

"Are you afraid?" I asked.

Harry shot me a look. "Me? Afraid? Come on!"

Then he whispered, "Make that five minutes in the Dungeon. Tell the teacher at 9:05."

I looked at the clock. It was 8:58.

"Okay, Harry," I whispered back.

It would be easier to tell on Song Lee if she wasn't there.

"Boys and girls," Miss Mackle said. "This is Mr. Kookhammer."

"Skooghammer," he corrected.

Everyone laughed except Harry.

Miss Mackle continued, "Mr. Skooghammer will unfortunately be taking Harry down to the Suspension Room for the whole day. I look forward to seeing Harry tomorrow, when he will have a better attitude."

Mary folded her arms. "I knew Harry

would be the first one to go from our room."

Mr. Skooghammer pulled on his red beard as he waited at the door. He didn't have his black bag with him. It was probably in *the Dungeon*.

Harry got up. He walked down the aisle like he was walking to his execution.

Slowly.

Carefully.

Miss Mackle handed him a pile of work. "I expect this to be done by three, Harry."

Harry raised his head as if to say "yes" like a tough guy.

Then he dropped the books and papers. Ida got out of her seat and helped him pick them up.

Finally, Harry was at the doorway

with his stuff. He was about two feet shorter than Skooghammer.

When Harry turned and gave me one last look, he held up five fingers. I felt so bad. My buddy was innocent. He was going to the Dungeon for a crime he didn't do.

And for what?

A big black bag that bulged?

I didn't think Harry cared about it anymore.

Trapped

At 9:01, the Bean Broadcast came on. Mr. Cardini read the names of the good Human Beans over the intercom.

When he mentioned Room 2B, everyone listened for their own name.

"Mary Berg for clearing off her lunch table without being asked.

"Ida Burrell for helping other people with their fraction math.

"Sidney La Fleur and Song Lee Park for sharing their lunches with someone who left his at home."

Sidney blurted out, "I gave him a giant

oatmeal cookie, a carrot slice, and—"

"Shhhh!" Miss Mackle shushed.

"Doug Hurtuk . . ."

When I heard my name, I leaned forward.

". . . for being a good sport when his kickball team lost. He was the first to get in line and shake hands."

I automatically looked over at Harry's seat. He would have given me a high five. But his seat was empty.

I looked at the clock.

It was 9:07!

The Bean Broadcast was still going on.

Poor Harry. He was too brave to cry, but I pictured him crying. Skooghammer was probably chaining him to his desk by now.

I kept waiting for the broadcast to end.

Finally, at 9:11, Mr. Cardini finished, and I jumped out of my seat to speak with Miss Mackle privately.

"Please sit down, Doug," Miss Mackle said. "I have some important news."

It took five minutes for the teacher to talk about our science clubs, about how the newspaper article would be in the paper tomorrow morning, and about how important it was for us to return all our library books.

9:21.

Harry was probably dying.

I was desperate. I had to see him. I raised two fingers to go to the bathroom.

Miss Mackle nodded. So I took off.

"Walk, please!" Mr. Cardini boomed when I dashed by his office.

I slowed down.

As soon as I got to the boys' bathroom, I looked around. No one was there. I looked down into the gym. It was empty.

As I hurried down the stairs into the gym, I could see the old music room door propped open.

There it was.

The Dungeon.

I tiptoed as I got closer. I couldn't peek

in, because Skooghammer might see me, but I could listen.

Eavesdrop.

I got as close to the Dungeon door as possible, and waited.

I only heard one voice.

Skooghammer's.

"It's sharp. It could prick you," he said.

I took a step back.

It was the mace.

He was probably going to use it on Harry and those two fifth-grade boys.

I raced back through the gym, and up the stairs. I made up my mind to tell the teacher. *Now!*

When I got to Room 2B, Song Lee and Mrs. Park were talking to Miss Mackle.

Oh no! I thought.

Song Lee was back.

I watched from my seat as they

talked. Maybe . . . maybe Song Lee was confessing.

I waited.

I looked at the clock. 9:44.

Finally, Mrs. Park left, and Song Lee sat down.

When Miss Mackle started reading *Bartholomew and the Oobleck,* I knew I had to do it.

Myself.

Tell the truth about Song Lee.

And spring Harry.

When I raised my hand, Miss Mackle shook her head. She hates to be interrupted during a read-aloud.

And so it was almost 10:30 before I got my big chance.

"Miss Mackle," I said.

"Yes, Doug?"

"I have something to say about what

happened yesterday with the butterflies."

Everyone looked at me.

Song Lee did, too.

Her eyes were watering.

"Eh . . ."

"Yes?"

"Song Lee . . ." There, I thought. I got
her name out.

"Yes?"

Song Lee put her head down on her desk.

"Song Lee . . . gave the butterflies . . . some sugar water."

"I know. She was my helper yesterday. They needed sweet water to grow stronger. We'll probably let them go at recess today."

When the class groaned, Miss Mackle added, "Freedom is important. Our butterflies are entitled to it. Do you know they have never seen a real tree? Or the sky, or grass?"

Freedom.

Harry was chained to his desk.

Maybe his fingers were bleeding again from that mace.

I had just sentenced my best friend to a day in the Dungeon.

As I watched the butterflies zigzag

through the air in their net cage, I thought of Harry.

He was just like those painted ladies.

He was trapped, too.

Freedom!

It was hard for me to concentrate on my schoolwork. I kept worrying about Harry.

He probably hated me.

I had let him down.

I couldn't tattle on Song Lee. I *never* tattle on a friend.

"I saw Harry and those two fifth-grade boys," Mary said at our lunch table.

"They were walking in a straight line with their lunch trays. They didn't say boo. They just followed that Mr. Skooghammer to the Suspension Room."

"How was Harry?" Song Lee asked. She wasn't eating much of her lunch.

"I didn't see his face, but his head was down."

Sidney crunched on a carrot slice. "Did he have a ball and chain tied to his feet?"

"No, Sidney," Mary groaned.

"Did Mr. Skooghammer have a whip?" I asked.

Mary made a face. "This is the nineties. You're talking about the Middle Ages and dungeons."

I picked at my beans with a fork, then set it down. I wasn't hungry.

Song Lee wasn't either. Her taco was still untouched.

That afternoon when we went out for recess, Miss Mackle carried the huge yellow net cage. We huddled around

48

her when she stopped on the grass near a lilac bush.

"Okay, here we go. Keep your eye on our five painted ladies."

Everyone watched Miss Mackle open the net cage.

"There goes one!" Sidney shouted. *"Up there in the tree."*

"There's one on the lilac bush!" Ida said.

"Look!" Dexter pointed. "Two are flitting in the air. Now they're resting on the top branch of that tree."

Everyone clapped and cheered. Then they ran to the kickball diamond.

I sat down on the grass. I didn't feel like playing.

When we returned to the classroom, Miss Mackle didn't bother hanging the net cage up again.

"Wait," I said. "There's still one in there. Look!"

Miss Mackle stood on a chair as she put the net cage back up. One butterfly was resting on a carnation.

"It's the handicapped one!" Sydney shouted.

"The one Harry touched!" Mary snapped.

Suddenly, Song Lee stood up.

Everyone could tell she was going to cry. "I touch butterfly wing, not Harry. Harry take the blame for me."

The class gasped.

Miss Mackle walked over to Song Lee's desk and crouched down.

She looked right at Song Lee. "I'm glad you told me."

Song Lee covered her eyes and cried. "Oh, I'm so sorry!"

"It really wasn't her fault," I said.

52

"She wasn't here when you made that announcement about not touching the wings."

"I know," Miss Mackle said. "Song Lee is always gentle with living things. And . . . she tells the truth."

This time, I thought, it just happened to be twenty-four hours later.

Everyone watched the teacher go to her desk and write a note.

"Please take this down to the Suspension Room, Doug, and bring Harry back."

"*Yes!*" I shouted. And I flew out the door.

This time Mr. Cardini didn't see me, so I kept running.

When I got downstairs to the gym, I could see that the Suspension Room door was closed.

I hurried by the kids taking turns walking on the balance beam.

Then I stopped at the far door and knocked.

Mr. Skooghammer answered, read the note, and let me in.

I took a quick look around.

One small room.

With no windows.

Just gray walls.

And a cement floor.

Signs said:

NO TALKING.

YOU MUST STAY IN YOUR SEAT AT ALL TIMES.

ONE BATHROOM BREAK IN THE MORNING AND IN THE AFTERNOON ONLY.

LUNCH WILL BE EATEN IN THIS ROOM. SILENTLY.

All those signs gave me the shivers!

Three boys were sitting at desks facing different walls.

Harry was one of them.

"Well, Harry," Mr. Skooghammer said. "You're free to go back to your class now."

When I looked at Harry, I expected a big smile and a high five.

But there was just a frown.

55

"Can't I stay until the bell, Mr. Skoog-hammer?" he asked. "Please?"

I couldn't believe my ears. Harry wanted to stay in this *Dungeon!*

"Look, Doug," Harry said. "I under-stand hard math now. We counted the spirals on a pineapple and on pine cones."

So that's what was prickly in Mr. Skooghammer's black bag! I thought.

"Mr. Skooghammer is studying to be a math teacher. He showed us all kinds of neat things. Did you know daisies usually have 21 or 34 petals? It's called the Fibonacci Sequence."

I looked at all the stuff on the table in the middle of the room. They sure did a lot of math.

"Mr. Skooghammer said we could play Catch-the-Stars at the end of the day because no one fooled around, and we all got our work done."

I noticed Mr. Skooghammer had a beanbag with stars on it in his hand.

I couldn't believe it.

Who else could have fun doing math in a dungeon but *Harry!*

He always did like horrible things.

When I got back to class, I handed Miss Mackle another note.

"He's staying until the bell?" Miss Mackle asked.

I nodded.

Then I looked at Song Lee. "Don't worry about Harry. He's fine."

Song Lee had the biggest smile. "Our handicapped butterfly is fine, too. He flew out window! He was just not ready for freedom yet."

I smiled.

Neither was Harry.